Reading Level ~~5k 4~~ 3rd grade

book

And to Think That I Saw It on MULBERRY STREET

By DR. SEUSS

A Vanguard Press Book

Random House 🏠 New York

For

Helene McC.

Mother of the One and Original

Marco

Visit us on the Web!
Seussville.com
randomhousekids.com

Educators and librarians, for a variety of teaching tools, visit us at
RHTeachersLibrarians.com

ISBN 978-0-375-97581-3

This special edition was printed for Kohl's Department Stores, Inc.
(for distribution on behalf of Kohl's Cares, LLC, its wholly owned subsidiary)
by Random House Children's Books, a division of Penguin Random House LLC, New York.

KOHL'S
Style 9780375975813
Factory Number 126509
Production Date 09/2016

MANUFACTURED IN CHINA
10 9 8 7 6 5 4 3 2 1

WHEN I leave home to walk to school,
Dad always says to me,
"Marco, keep your eyelids up
And see what you can see."

But when I tell him where I've been
And what I think I've seen,
He looks at me and sternly says,
"Your eyesight's much too keen.

"Stop telling such outlandish tales.
Stop turning minnows into whales."

Now, what can I say
When I get home today?

Paige

1

All the long way to school
And all the way back,
I've looked and I've looked
And I've kept careful track,
But all that I've noticed,
Except my own feet,
Was a horse and a wagon
On Mulberry Street.

page 2

That's nothing to tell of,
That won't do, of course . . .
Just a broken-down wagon
That's drawn by a horse.

That *can't* be my story. That's only a *start*.
I'll say that a ZEBRA was pulling that cart!
And that is a story that no one can beat,
When I say that I saw it on Mulberry Street.

Page 3

Yes, the zebra is fine,
But I think it's a shame,
Such a marvelous beast
With a cart that's so tame.
The story would really be better to hear
If the driver I saw were a charioteer.
A gold and blue chariot's *something* to meet,
Rumbling like thunder down Mulberry Street!

page 4

No, it won't do at all . . .
A zebra's too small.

page 5

A reindeer is better;
He's fast and he's fleet,

page 6

And he'd look mighty smart
On old Mulberry Street.

Hold on a minute!
There's something wrong!

page 7

A reindeer hates the way it feels
To pull a thing that runs on wheels.

Page

He'd be much happier, instead,
If he could pull a fancy sled.

Hmmmm . . . A reindeer and sleigh . . .

Say—*any*one could think of *that,*
Jack or Fred or Joe or Nat—
Say, even Jane could think of *that.*

Page 9

But it isn't too late to make one little change.
A sleigh and an ELEPHANT! *There's* something strange!

I'll pick one with plenty of power and size,
A blue one with plenty of fun in his eyes.
And then, just to give him a little more tone,
Have a Rajah, with rubies, perched high on a throne.

Page 10

Say! That makes a story that *no one* can beat,
When I say that I saw it on Mulberry Street.

But now I don't know . . .
It still doesn't seem right.

page 11

An elephant pulling a thing that's so light
Would whip it around in the air like a kite.

page 12

But he'd look simply grand
With a great big brass band!

page 13

A band that's so good should have someone to hear it,
But it's going so fast that it's hard to keep near it.
I'll put on a trailer! I know they won't mind
If a man sits and listens while hitched on behind.

Page 14

But now is it fair? Is it fair what I've done?
I'll bet those wagons weigh more than a ton.
That's really too heavy a load for *one* beast;
I'll give him some helpers. He needs two, at least.

But now what worries me is this . . .
Mulberry Street runs into Bliss,

page 15

Unless there's something I can fix up,
There'll be an *awful* traffic mix-up!

Page 16

It takes Police to do the trick,
To guide them through where traffic's thick—
It takes Police to do the trick.

page 17

They'll never crash now. They'll race at top speed
With Sergeant Mulvaney, himself, in the lead.

page   18

The Mayor is there
And he thinks it is grand,
And he raises his hat
As they dash by the stand.

page 19

The Mayor is there
And the Aldermen too,
All waving big banners
Of red, white and blue.

And that is a story that NO ONE can beat
When I say that I saw it on Mulberry Street!

Page 20

With a roar of its motor an airplane appears
And dumps out confetti while everyone cheers.

And that makes a story that's really not bad!
But it still could be better. Suppose that I add . . . .

page 22

. . . A Chinese man
Who eats with sticks. . . .

A big Magician
Doing tricks. . . .

A ten-foot beard
That needs a comb. . . .

No time for more,
I'm almost home.

I swung 'round the corner
And dashed through the gate,
I ran up the steps
And I felt simply GREAT!

FOR I HAD A STORY THAT **NO ONE** COULD BEAT!
AND TO THINK THAT I SAW IT ON MULBERRY STREET!

page 25

But Dad said quite calmly,
"Just draw up your stool
And tell me the sights
On the way home from school."

There was so much to tell, I JUST COULDN'T BEGIN!
Dad looked at me sharply and pulled at his chin.
He frowned at me sternly from there in his seat,
"Was there nothing to look at . . . no people to greet?
Did *nothing* excite you or make your heart beat?"

page 26

"Nothing," I said, growing red as a beet,
"But a plain horse and wagon on Mulberry Street."

page 27